HELP!

MY DINOSAURS ARE
LOST IN THE CITY!

Forgive me for such a silly blunder... where could they be, i wonder?

Where's SPIKE?

The first one is easy... there's only **one to find.**

Can you spot him, **if you'd be so kind?**

Where are
CHOMP & GRIFF?

One is **quiet,**
the other is
LOUD...

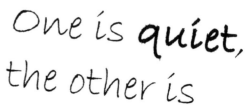

both are **lost amongst**
the crowd!

where are **BITZY** & **DINKY?**

One is yellow like a **rubber duck...**

the other likes to stomp in **muddy muck!**

where are PICKLES & TAG?

These two
are in the
playground...

but, I wonder, can
they be found?

Where are TRIXIE & DASH?

One has an orange tail...

the other's slower than a cheetah, but **faster than a snail!**

where are BABBLE & DOT?

One likes to collect shiny things...

the other likes to flap their wings!

Where are AXEL & MR BITEY?

These two are a little bit shy...

they're in an office, high in the sky!

where are RORY & GRIZZA?

One is a lovely shade of **red**...

the other is brown, with **horns on its head!**

Where are

TITUS & PETRI?

One has a brother called Larry...

the other has an uncle called Barry!

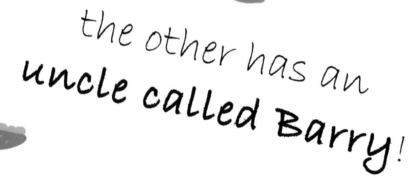

DANGER
SLIPPERY ICE!

Where are DINGO & STEGGY?

These two are friends, they're a **cute little** pair...

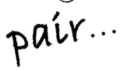

I think they've gone to the **funfair**!

Where are ROXY & GERTIE?

One is scared of the dark...

the other is scared of dogs, especially when they **bark**!

where are DEENA & KIRKY?

He is orange,
she is pink...

let's find them both,
what do you think?

where are BLINKY & PINCH?

This pair like to stay **healthy and slim**...

...so you might find them in the **city gym!**

Where are STOMPY & RAPPA?

These two are hiding, and both are rare...

they are the **last to find**... have you seen them **anywhere**?

THANK YOU!

The dinosaurs have been found...
Now they're coming back home,
all safe and sound!

A Bonus Search

BABY DINOSAURS!

The three below are hiding in
the book. Don't believe me?
Go take a look!

THE END!

Find us on Amazon!

Discover all of the titles available in the series;
including these below...

HELP! I'VE LOST MY TEDDIES!

HELP! MY ROBOTS ARE LOST IN THE CITY!

HELP! THERE'S AN ANIMAL THIEF ON THE LOOSE!

HELP! MY MONSTERS ARE ON THE LOOSE!

HELP! MY FRIENDS HAVE GONE MISSING!

HELP! THE PIRATE HAS LOST HIS SHIPMATES!

Printed in Great Britain
by Amazon